What Frank Watched

by Rosie Bensen

illustrated by Manuel King

Scott Foresman

Editorial Offices: Glenview, Illinois • New York, New York
Sales Offices: Reading, Massachusetts • Duluth, Georgia
Glenview, Illinois • Carrollton, Texas • Menlo Park, California

Frank's brother Steve had a TV repair business. One day, he gave Frank a television set.

"I want to share the wealth!" he explained to Frank.

Frank had never had a TV. His friends came over to see it.

"Nice set," Marsha said.

"Big screen," Lindy said.

"You'll love it!" Steve said.

"There is a wealth of good shows!"

That night, Frank watched his television. But he didn't see anything interesting.

The next day, Lindy called.
"How is the new set?" she asked.
"Fine," Frank said.

That night Frank watched his
television again. He watched and he
watched. He hoped to see something
really clever. But he did not.

Steve called the next morning.

"Hi, Frank. Did you watch your new television?" he asked.

"I sure did," Frank told him.

"I knew you'd like it," Steve said.

Frank really wanted to like TV.
All his friends did.

So that night he watched again.
He watched, and watched, and watched
some more. He was sure that this time
he would see something amazing.

No such luck.

Bird
Baths
For Fun
& Profit

Marsha called next.

"Frank, be sure to watch TV tonight. There is a mystery on," Marsha said. "It's called 'Which Business Was Cheated?'"

"I love clever mysteries," Frank said. "I'll watch it."

That night, Frank watched his TV.
He watched it until he fell asleep in front
of the screen.

Frank thought maybe he was just being lazy. He made up his mind to try harder. He would watch TV until he learned how to enjoy it. All his friends could not be wrong.

The next night, he sat down in front of the set again.

That's when Marsha and Steve and
Lindy came to visit.

"What are you watching, Frank?"
they asked.

"Nothing," Frank said, feeling
lazy again.

"Nothing?" they all asked.

Marsha looked at the sct.

She looked at Frank.

Then she looked at the set again.

"Frank," she said. "It works better if you turn it on."

"Oops!" said Frank.

"I guess you didn't see that clever mystery last night," Lindy said.

"Well, no," said Frank. "But I do know a good mystery . . . in a book."

"What is it about?" Steve asked.

Frank blushed. "A missing television," he said.

"Great! May I borrow it?" Lindy asked.

"May I have it next?" Steve asked.

"How do I get to the library?" Marsha asked.

That night everyone enjoyed a good mystery.